STERLING and the distinctive Sterling logo are
registered trademarks of Sterling Publishing Co., Inc.

Library of Congress Cataloging-in-Publication Data

Wax, Wendy (Wendy Anne)
Arlo makes a friend / by Wendy Wax ; illustrated by Adam Relf.
p. cm.
Summary: While exploring his new neighborhood, Arlo, an armadillo, makes friends
with rabbit as the two stand together against a snake who is a bully.
ISBN 978-1-4027-4726-7
[1. Friendship--Fiction. 2. Bullies--Fiction. 3. Moving, Household--Fiction. 4. Armadillos--Fiction.
5. Snakes--Fiction. 6. Rabbits--Fiction.] I. Relf, Adam, ill. II. Title.

PZ7.W35117Arl 2008
[E]--dc22
2007043485

2 4 6 8 10 9 7 5 3 1

Published by Sterling Publishing Co., Inc.
387 Park Avenue South, New York, NY 10016
www.sterlingpublishing.com/kids
Text © 2008 by Wendy Wax
Illustrations © 2008 by Adam Relf
Designed by Lauren Rille
Distributed in Canada by Sterling Publishing
C/o Canadian Manda Group, 165 Dufferin Street, Toronto, Ontario, Canada M6K 3H6
Distributed in the United Kingdom by GMC Distribution Services,
Castle Place, 166 High Street, Lewes, East Sussex, England BN7 1XU
Distributed in Australia by Capricorn Link (Australia) Pty. Ltd.,
P.O. Box 704, Windsor, NSW 2756, Australia

Sterling ISBN 978-1-4027-4726-7

For information about custom editions, special sales, premium and corporate purchases, please contact
Sterling Special Sales Department at 800-805-5489 or specialsales@sterlingpublishing.com.

Arlo Makes a Friend

by
Wendy Wax

illustrated by
Adam Relf

STERLING

New York / London

Arlo the armadillo spent the first morning in his new home helping his parents settle in.

"Let's go out and explore!" he said after lunch.
But his mom and dad were too busy.
So Arlo set off alone.
He missed his friends and wished he
hadn't moved so far away from them.

Suddenly, Arlo saw something
red and yellow flying toward him.
It was a mango!
Just before it hit him . . .

. . . he rolled his hard shell into a ball.

CLuNk!

Arlo felt cozy and safe inside his shell.
Then two more mangos fell!

THuD!

ThUd!

Arlo poked his nose out.
He smelled something—
or someone—nearby.

There was a snake in the mango tree above him!
At first Arlo stayed hidden,
but that soon became boring.
"I'll never make friends in my shell,"
he thought. "Maybe the snake is nice."
Arlo unrolled himself and looked up.

"Hello," Arlo said shyly.

"Hello yourself," said the snake.
"Want to see something funny?"

Not waiting for an answer,
the snake shook the branch and
more mangos fell.

CLUNK! CLUNK! CLUNK!

They landed on Arlo's hard shell.
This time Arlo didn't roll up and hide.
He wasn't going to let a mean snake ruin his day!

Arlo took a deep breath.
"Will you please stop shaking
that branch?" he asked.
The snake shook the branch harder,
sending mangos flying everywhere.

THuD! ThUd!
CLunK!

"Well, well, well! Time to hide in
your shell, shell, shell!"
sang the snake.

But Arlo didn't hide.

He began to dig.
Not only was Arlo an expert digger,
digging was his favorite thing to do.
He dug so quickly, the snake forgot
all about shaking branches and just stared.

Within minutes, Arlo had dug out
a deep burrow.
But he didn't stop there—
he was having too much fun digging!

Arlo soon forgot all about the snake.
He was busy digging around roots, pushing
stones, pulling weeds, and tossing twigs aside.
Arlo whistled while he worked until—

THuMP!

He bumped into a rabbit!

"Hey, watch it!" said the rabbit, who
   had been digging in the other direction.

"Sorry," said Arlo. "But I ..."

"You have to move," said the rabbit.

 Arlo started to move but then stopped.
"Who says?" he asked.

"I do," said the rabbit.

"Well I say *no*," said Arlo, sounding braver than he felt.

The rabbit refused to budge.
So did Arlo.
Arlo had put a lot of work into his tunnel,
and he wasn't going to let a rabbit take it over.
Now he missed his old friends more than ever.

"Hello!" hissed a voice from above.
Arlo shuddered at the sound. The rabbit did too.

It was the snake!

Feeling trapped between a mean snake and a bossy rabbit, Arlo rolled into a ball.

"How did you do that?" asked the rabbit.
Arlo didn't bother to answer him.

The rabbit came closer. "Are you okay in there?" he asked.

"What does it matter to you?" Arlo mumbled,
feeling sorry for himself.

"Well … there are two of us in here and only one snake out there," said the rabbit. "Two are stronger than one … as you probably know."

The rabbit sounded nicer than before.

Arlo unrolled himself.

"I'm Arlo, and I'm new around here," Arlo said shyly.

"I'm Jack," said the rabbit. "I'll show you around
  the forest."

Arlo liked that idea.

"Hello!" the snake called again.

"That's Boris," said Jack. "He's a bully."

"He hit me with mangos," said Arlo. "That's why I came down here."

"Let's stick together," said Jack. "We can turn our two tunnels into a hideout."

"Boris will never find us!" added Arlo.

Jack took Arlo on a tour of his side of the tunnel.
"Great job!" said Arlo.

Then Arlo showed Jack his side of the tunnel.
"I'm impressed!" said Jack.

The new friends made plans to add more secret tunnels.

It was getting late.

"Let's meet here tomorrow
so we can keep digging," said Arlo.

"I can't wait!" said Jack.

The two friends left the tunnel together—
just in case Boris was still around.

Sure enough, Boris was still in the mango tree— but he had fallen asleep!

Arlo and Jack tiptoed by him as quietly as they could. But suddenly, Arlo stepped on a twig.

CrACk!

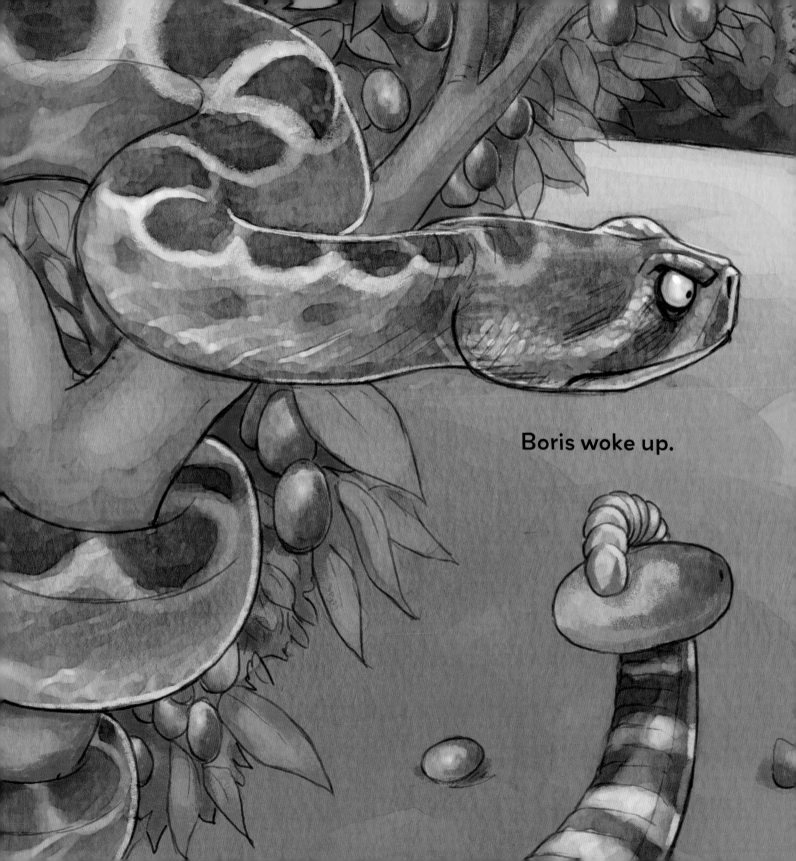

Boris woke up.

"Look who's back for a mango snack!" said Boris.

"I *am* back," said Arlo bravely. "With Jack!"

Boris shook a branch and mangos flew everywhere.

Quick as lightning, Jack used his large feet to kick the mangos back up at Boris.

ThUd!
THuD!
ThUD!

"Ouch! Ouch! Ouch!" shouted Boris.

Boris slithered down the tree and slunk away. "Nice work, Jack," called Arlo. Then he rolled himself into a tight ball, nudged himself forward, and began to roll toward home.

Down,
down,
down Arlo went, right to the entrance of his burrow.

Safe at home, Arlo told his mom and dad all about his day. He barely mentioned Boris and the mangos. It was much more fun talking about his new friend.